THE FLOWER FAERIE

by Frank Asch and Vladimir Vagin

SCHOLASTIC INC.

New York

Library of Congress Cataloging-in-Publication Data
Asch, Frank.
The flower faerie / by Frank Asch ; illustrated by Vladimir Vagin.
p. cm.
Summary: The Emperor's son comes to the aid of a Faerie whom the
Emperor has captured and placed in a display case.
ISBN 0-590-45493-5
[1. Fairy tales.] I. Vagin, Vladimir Vasil'evich, 1937–   ill.
II. Title.
PZ8.A893Fl   1992
[E]—dc20   91-33763   CIP
AC
12 11 10 9 8 7 6 5 4 3 2   3 4 5 6 7/9
Printed in the U.S.A.   36

First Scholastic printing, March 1993

This artwork was painted
with dyes, gouache and
watercolor.

To all my good friends
in the beautiful state of Vermont
—*Vladimir Vagin*

To Lazaris and all my friends
at Concept Synergy
—*Frank Asch*

NE DAY in early spring an Emperor's son stole away from his fencing lesson and went for a walk in the forest. As usual he carried his paint box, hoping to find some interesting subject to draw or paint. At first nothing captured his eye, but as he entered the deepest, darkest part of the forest, he saw a large yellow flower that seemed to be glowing with a light from within. Slowly he edged closer. Peering down inside the beautiful blossom, he saw a magical being made of rainbow-colored light: a sleeping Faerie with golden hair, and features as delicate as mist.

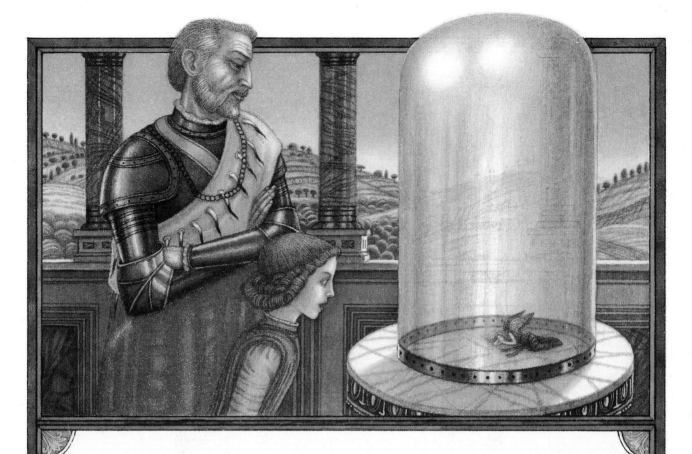

The Emperor's son wanted to reach out and touch the Faerie. But he dared not disturb such a wondrous creature. With trembling hands he picked up his brush and began to paint her picture.

He had hardly begun when his father appeared.

"I thought I'd find you here!" bellowed the Emperor. "Your fencing instructor has been searching the palace for you!"

Then the Emperor spied the Faerie. Like his son he was taken with her beauty. Without a moment's hesitation he reached down and plucked the large yellow flower.

"Father! What are you doing?" cried his son.

The Emperor made no reply. He carried the flower back to his palace and commanded his servants to seal the slumbering Faerie in a glass case.

With an uneasy feeling the Emperor's son watched over the Faerie while she slept. When she awoke he greeted her with a gentle whisper. "Please don't be afraid," he said. "My father means you no harm." But the Faerie would not be comforted. She stood up and, spreading her wings, hurled herself against the glass.

"Father, can't you see? The Faerie's not happy here! We must take her back to the forest where she belongs."

"My palace is where she belongs," replied the Emperor.

He ordered his servants to bring the Faerie a chest filled with emeralds, rubies, and gold. The Faerie hardly glanced at the Emperor's offering.

"I don't think Faeries care much for treasure," said the Emperor's son. "They like flowers."

The Emperor nodded. "Yes, of course!" He instructed his servants to surround the Faerie with baskets of beautiful flowers.

After many vain attempts to escape, the Faerie finally gave up.

"You see, she's happy now," said the Emperor. Thoroughly pleased with himself, he sent out word of the Faerie's capture and prepared to greet hoards of admiring visitors.

"How lovely!" they exclaimed as one by one they filed past the forlorn Faerie. "Just exquisite!" "What a gem!"

When the flowers surrounding the Faerie began to wither, she seemed to grow weak. Noticing this, the Emperor sent his servants to fetch more flowers. "If necessary pick every flower in the kingdom!"

The servants dutifully obeyed the Emperor's command. But each time they returned to the palace with fewer flowers and disturbing news.

"The apple trees are not blooming this year," said the gardeners who tended the Emperor's orchards. "Without blossoms there will be no fruit."

"Without flowers the bees can make no honey," said the beekeepers.

And the farmers complained that if their gardens and fields did not flower soon there would be nothing to harvest in the fall.

One day the Emperor's servants returned to the palace empty-handed.

"There is not a single flower to be found in your entire kingdom," they reported. "The people are gathering outside the palace walls in protest. They say that without the help of your Faerie their crops will fail and their children will starve. They demand you release her at once."

"What nonsense!" sputtered the Emperor. "Send the people home with this warning: Those who attempt to steal my precious Faerie will pay with their lives!"

The Emperor gave the ailing Faerie to his royal physicians and told them, "Make her well, or else!"

The physicians did their best, but without flowers to keep her healthy the Faerie grew weaker every day. The glow vanished from her cheeks. Her wings became brittle. Her skin turned pale and powdery.

In despair the Emperor's son begged his father to let the Faerie go. "I'm afraid she'll die," he pleaded. But the Emperor's mind was made up. "I'll never let her go!" he insisted.

So late one night, while the royal household slept, the Emperor's son silently lifted the glass case, cradled the Faerie's limp body in his hands, and carried her back to the forest.

"At last, you are free!" he whispered to the Faerie, but she was too weak to fly.

Only a flower could save her now, thought the Emperor's son.

As he watched the Faerie gasp for breath he mournfully recalled the first time he saw her. "I just wanted to paint her portrait." He sighed to himself. Then he remembered the paper and tiny box of paints that he always carried with him.

He took out his brush and, by the light of the moon, began to paint a picture of the most beautiful flower he could imagine.

When his painting was done he placed it beside the Faerie.
All of a sudden her eyelids began to flutter. Slowly the color
flowed back into her cheeks. She stood up, raised her iridescent
wings, and began to fly.

Though the forest was still dark, the Emperor's son felt as if the sun were shining inside him.

Just then a band of his father's soldiers appeared.

"There he is! Grab him!" they yelled. The Emperor's son ran for his life. But the soldiers seemed to come from every direction. They ran him down like hounds chasing a rabbit.

When they caught him they locked him in the tall grim tower that was the palace prison.

As the prison door clanged shut the Emperor's son heard the sound of someone sobbing. Turning, he saw a hunched figure in the shadows. There is something so familiar about that voice, he thought.

Then he realized the sobbing figure was his own father!

"The people have taken over the kingdom and sentenced us to death!" cried the Emperor. "What a fool I was! Can you ever forgive me?" He reached out to embrace his son.

At that moment the Faerie, strengthened by her night in the forest, soared toward the palace. As she flew over the now

barren land, every flowering plant in the kingdom opened its blossoms to greet her.

When the Faerie reached the palace tower the small vine growing at its base burst into bloom and grew all the way up the tower to the prison window. The Emperor and his son ran to the window and grabbed hold of the vine.

Then they lowered themselves down to the ground and fled.

For weeks and weeks they hid themselves in the forest, sleeping in a hollow tree and surviving on roots and berries.

While they hid, the fruit trees bloomed and the bees made honey. With the help of the Flower Faerie, the harvest proved to be plentiful. In the fall, the people of the kingdom forgave the Emperor and allowed him to return to the palace.

From then on the Emperor ruled wisely. He never tried to
recapture the Faerie. With his own hands he planted a beautiful
garden in her honor. Often he and his son took long walks in
the forest to visit with the Faerie. And sometimes she came to
the palace to visit with them.